Auntie Betty baby

Bet that's →
baby spit-up. GROSS ME OUT

Dear Dilly,

By now Daddy has told you that your brother Matthew was born last night. Isn't that exciting news?! Daddy thinks he looks a lot like Auntie Betty.

I'm giving you this diary as a big sister present so you can write down your feelings. (You can write down interesting things about Matthew, too!)

Even though you will be coming to visit us in the hospital tomorrow, I'll send this home with Daddy so you can start using it right away!

Love,
Mom

P.S. You will be a wonderful big sister!
P.P.S. Here's a kiss for you!

what a Cutie! How old is she? 92? Aawww...

Goo Goo Ga Ga

I have never heard of "P.P.S." Did they just invent it?

This is <u>not</u> a two-headed boy.?

This one is Gary →

...and this one is John

For John and Gary (even though boys are GROSS!!)
(and <u>endearing</u> little brothers everywhere)

↓

Puh-<u>LEEZ</u>

This lady is <u>so</u>, <u>so</u> nice, really she is

Many, many thanks to Amy Shields for her inspirational ideas and her guidance and support.

Library of Congress Cataloging-in-Publication Data
Lewis, Cynthia Copeland, 1960—
Dilly's big sister diary / Cynthia Copeland Lewis.
p.   cm.

Summary: When her brother Matthew is born Dilly's parents give her a diary to record her feelings about him, and over the course of two months Dilly begins to change her mind about being a big sister.
ISBN 0-7613-0414-2 (lib. bdg.) 0-7613-0441-X (trade)
(1. Brothers and sisters—Fiction. 2. Babies—Fiction. 3. Diaries—Fiction.] I. Title.

PZ7.L584755Di 1998
[Fic]—dc21   97-47431   CIP   AC

I DO NOT!

But you have to call her "Cindy" because she hates being called "Cynthia."

← This is her, many, many moons ago.

SHHH! This is a SECRET MESSAGE like... URA B-U-T!

Published by The Millbrook Press
2 Old New Milford Road
Brookfield, Connectcut 06804

(I M 2!)

Dilly's

Don't you dare peek

BIG SISTER

Keep out or ELSE

Diary

by Dilly, of course
by Dilly
by Dilly

Isn't my mom a cutie pie? :)

me and Mom right before YOU-KNOW-WHO came along and WRECKED EVERYTHING!!

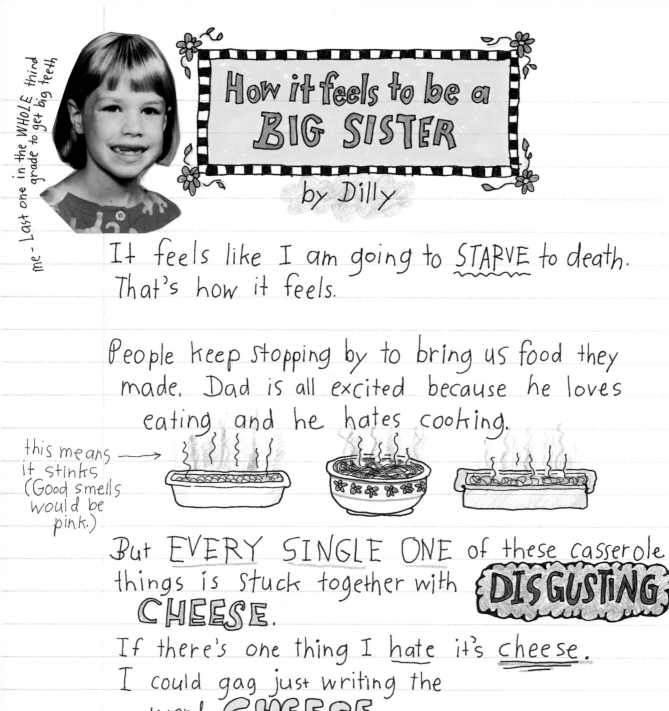

me - Last one in the WHOLE third grade to get big teeth

How it feels to be a BIG SISTER

by Dilly

It feels like I am going to STARVE to death. That's how it feels.

People keep stopping by to bring us food they made. Dad is all excited because he loves eating and he hates cooking.

this means → it stinks (Good smells would be pink.)

But EVERY SINGLE ONE of these casserole things is stuck together with DISGUSTING CHEESE.

If there's one thing I hate it's cheese.

I could gag just writing the word CHEESE.

"GAG" See?!

If my mother was home, my bows would match my shirt.

♥Note Mom taped to my bathroom mirror the night she went to the hospital ♥ ⟶

The next time we see each other, you will be a BIG SISTER!!
♡ Mom

Dad and I
~~Dad and me~~
~~Me and Dad~~ just got back from the hospital. This is what Mom's room looks like:

← (this is a pillow, not a flag)

The bed moves if you push the buttons

(I forgot what this part of the bed looks like)

T.V. clicker

Blah Blah Blah

← TV hangs on the wall and gets, like, 1,000,000,000 channels

A nice lady brings Mom's dinner on a tray just like the hot lunch at school (except she gets to watch T.V. while she eats).

Maybe she won't even want to come home.

F.Y.I.*

thumbs down!

Well, Matthew is DEFINITELY NOT what I wanted.

Everyone says how cute he is. Boy, if he's a cute baby, I'd sure hate to see an ugly one.

*F.Y.I. means "For Your Information." Dad told me that.

I checked out the nursery just to see if there were any cute babies and maybe we could trade. But they all looked red and squished. The whole batch came out punky. (I love the word **PUNKY.** Mom uses it when something is not quite right. Punky smell, Punky waffles, PUNKY MATTHEW.)

This afternoon, Dad helped me make BIG SISTER announcements. Here's one:

BABY BROTHER!

Dilly Duncan is now a BIG SISTER to Matthew John Duncan

8 pounds and 22 inches

Born at 8:30 p.m. on April 23rd

List of who I will send them to:

1. Meredith (best friend) →
2. Annie (second best)
3. Cammy (likes bunnies, does monkey bars with me at recess)
4. ~~Kate~~ NOT UNTIL SHE GIVES ME BACK MY SNAKE RING!
5. Jeffrey (cousin, Dad said I had to) ↘
6. Beanie (neighbor)

← pierced ears— LUCKY!!

GOOFY, Like ALL BOYS!

Beans, beans, the musical fruit, the more you eat, the more you toot! (Dad taught me that)

Daddy told me to put a postcard (with my address and a stamp on it) in each envelope. He said my friends will write back and I'll get mail! I bet Meredith will write first.

We interrupt this diary to bring you a SPECIAL ANNOUNCEMENT!

> **MOM COMES HOME TOMORROW!!**
> (NO MORE CHEESY FOOD!)

First thing today Dad asked me to record a message on the answering machine about the new baby. At first I didn't want to, but then Dad promised he'd let me steer the car down the street later, so I said OK.

(FIRST MESSAGE— I did it alone)

answering machine →

> Hi! You've reached the Duncans, now including Punky Matthew. He is all squished and red and has a pointy head. Bye!

I thought it was good, but Dad erased it and wrote down some dopey stuff for me to read.

> Hello. The Duncans are happy to announce the birth of Matthew. He was born on Sunday, and weighed 8 pounds. Mother and baby AND BIG SISTER are doing fine. Leave us a message. Bye.

me, falling asleep listening to my B-O-O-O-RING message

ZZZ

drool

ZZZZ

our dog — if we had one — falling asleep too

If I were G + H, I'd get pretty mad about having to show up to be in all these words and being SILENT!
↓

BRI**GH**T
NI**GH**TLI**GH**T
(ooh— double whammy!!)

LAU**GH**
(Hey! F got to speak and he isn't even here!)

I just hope none of my friends like Meredith or Annie calls when we're gone.

TOp SeCReT MeSsAGE

(hint: "HISS") — H + M

WELCOME HOME!

Sign me and Dad made at the office

The GOOD NEWS ~~~> Mom came home today!

YEA!

me, cheering →

The BAD NEWS ~~~> She brought Matthew with her.

BOOOO!

I thought it might be kind of fun to hold him even though he is all pinchy and squished looking. BUT EVERYBODY KEPT TELLING ME WHAT TO DO!

→ "Sit here with a pillow on your lap!"
→ "Don't let his head flop around!"
→ "Don't let him roll off!"

balloons me and Dad DAD AND I tied to the mailbox

A BOY IT'S A BO BOY!

WHAT DO THEY THINK? I'M GOING TO HOLD HIM LIKE THIS?

Dead skunk hold   OR   Towel hold   OR   Hat hold

Nice hat!

Thanks.

Plus, he was so squirmy it was like holding a pile of jello.

Today Dad bought me a <u>BIG</u> <u>SISTER</u> present
—an instant camera so I could take
my own pictures of the baby. (Actually, it <u>is</u>
pretty cool the way they come out of the
camera right away.)

whoopee.

← cute little girl in the park that I would rather have instead of Matthew

My beautiful mother and NEVER MIND.

Nice living room floor (Oh, and the always happy Matthew)

My dog. (OK, OK, it's Beanie's dog but I like to pretend it's mine)

Hey Matthew— Roses are red, Violets are blue, Umbrellas get lost, so why don't <u>YOU</u>?!

I LOVE
HAVING
MOM HOME
BUT IT'S JUST NOT THE SAME.

BULLETIN:

Dad actually learned to make MEATLOAF! Yummy! 😋

I read him the directions out of the cookbook and after dinner we cleaned up the kitchen together. It was kind of fun because Dad does everything in an UN-MOM sort of way. (Like, he put the plates on the porch for Beanie's dog to lick before we put them in the dishwasher.)

I KNEW Meredith's postcard would be the first one to come! ↘

Lick Lick

This is not a pig. It is Beanie's dog.

Meredith loves chickens so she always draws them. She wants an alive one but she lives in a condo with no real yard so she has a gerbil named "Mr. Chicken."

Dear Dilly,
Sorry about your new brother. Bet he gets all the attention, huh. That's what my cousin told me.
I hope I can still come play on Saturday or do you have to be changing diapers and wiping spit-up now. Let me know.
Love your best friend forever, Meredith

USA 20

TO:
DILLY DUNCAN
18 ACREBROOK RD.
LITCHFIELD, CT
06759

Mom and Dad are all excited about coming up with a nickname for PRECIOUS Matthew... 😐

How about Matty? Or just plain Matt?

Or M.J. for Matthew John?

Or how about Matth PEW cuz he stinks!
(This is the way my babysitter Carrie writes "because." She also writes "luv" for "LOVE" and "thx" instead of "THANKS." She's cool.)

MatthPEW napped practically the whole day today so I had to be QUIET. SHHH Mom said to do puzzles so I dumped out 3 and mixed up all of the pieces to make it harder. But then it was TOO hard. Mom came and helped me. It was like old times! THEN old MatthPEW woke up bawling and RUINED EVERYTHING!

When Dad came home from work he brought a couple thousand THRILLING pictures of MatthPEW from the photo store.

MatthPEW sleeping!   MatthPEW yawning!   MatthPEW looking!   MatthPEW napping!   MatthPEW bawling!

LOOK— If the kid goes BUNGIE JUMPING, I'll be the first one to snap a picture. But SLEEPING?? Come ON!

I must have looked a little bummed out cuz Dad went and got a photo album from when I was a baby! There were ZILLIONS of pictures—Dilly napping, Dilly looking, Dilly yawning, Dilly sleeping... They were very interesting. Mom let ← me have this one. ☺

DILLY 11-8-89

(I look a little PUNKY here myself. I wonder why Mom and Dad look so happy. Weren't they worried I might have that pointy head FOREVER?)

MEREDITH CAME OVER TODAY!

(This is a chicken's waddle) →

← (Meredith drew these chickens!)

Mom said she could come over if we played outside or QUIETLY inside. Meredith said at her house she NEVER has to be quiet if she doesn't want to. We decided to play MAD SCIENTISTS and experiment on MatthPEW. (Meredith took notes like a real scientist.)

LOTS OF BRIGHT IDEAS

Experiment #1. Rub baby's palm with finger. RESULT: Baby will grab finger!

Experiment #2. Rub bottom of baby's foot near toes. RESULT: Baby's toes grab finger!

Experiment #3. Stroke baby's left cheek. RESULT: Baby turns to his left. (Ditto right cheek.) Baby thinks it is time to nurse.

Experiment #4. Ring doorbell near baby. RESULT: Baby jerks around.

This is a REAL scientist, Albert Einstein. (I traced it out of my science book.) He was so busy doing experiments he had no time to comb his hair.

:(I was sad when Meredith had to go.

SUPER ★ SECRETS

★ Sometimes I want to take Matt's fat little arm and pinch it until he cries.

★ I took the stuffed shark Auntie Betty gave Matt and hid it under my bed because I really like sharks and anyway he has too much stuff.

★ When no one was looking I climbed into Matt's crib (OR SHOULD I SAY MY CRIB CUZ IT WAS MINE FIRST!!) I felt like a lion in a cage at the zoo. I like my bunk beds better.

NO PEEKING

Dad thought it was interesting about us being mad scientists. He had an experiment he wanted to try! I sat on one side of Matt and he sat on the other. First he talked and then I did. Matt turned toward me! Dad said babies like high voices more than low ones.

WHAT I LEARNED TODAY → Being <u>8</u> is OK.
(Read on...)

What a **FUN SUNDAY!** (Almost like before <u>Matth PEW</u>.) Dad took me out for mini golf and ice cream. After he let me win, he bought me a hot fudge sunday with **3** CHERRIES and a ton of gummy bears 🐻 on top! Then we went to Dad's office. We brought my bike and Dad let me ride it up and down the halls. As we were leaving, Dad said, "Just think! Matt's <u>way</u> too little to do any of the things <u>WE</u> did today!"

Heading straight for the hole!

OTHER STUFF BABIES CAN'T DO

1. Cartwheels ←What's this? (A caterpillar doing a cartwheel!)
2. Read the funnies in the paper
3. Play chess (OK, neither can I, but at least <u>I</u> know what chess <u>IS</u>)
4. Do the monkey bars, skipping one
5. Go to the movies
6. Jump on Beanie's trampoline
7. Order a hot fudge sunday (with 3 cherries and gummy bears)

STUFF BABIES CAN DO

1. Poop in their diapers (Yummy)
2. Drink milk and spit it up.
3. Bawl their heads off cuz no one knows what they want. (Luckies!)
4. Look at the same dumb baby toys all day long
5. Get held all the time even when they're sick of it

me, hoping I don't get stuck sitting next to one of Beanie's goofy brothers

BUS STOP

new buses with no noses →

Meredith gave me GIPs in line TWICE and half her Skittles cuz Mom forgot to pack my dessert. She's REALLY my best friend!

Today was my first day back at school after Spring Vacation and my Special BIG SISTER vacation (well, that was ONE good thing MatthPEW did for me). Everyone made a big deal about it. Blah, blah, blah...

Mom made some "It's a boy!" pencils. (IT is right.)

IT'S A BOY

Mrs. Bunn, my teacher, said I could pass them out at snack. I gave 2 to Sam Horton (EVEN THOUGH I CAN'T STAND HIM) because I knew he'd put them up his nose and get in trouble WHICH HE DID. hee hee hee I wouldn't hate him so much if he didn't bring cheese for snack every single day.

→ Our class is planning a Mother's Day Tea. On Friday, the mothers will all come at 11:00 for iced tea and cookies. Today we made placemats. Meredith drew chickens on hers. I drew a lovely picture of Mom smiling B.M.
(Before Matthew)

↑ This is hot tea. Ours will be iced.

Beets

TRASH

(At dinner I realized that having Matt around is OK cuz Mom and Dad are so busy jiggling him around so he won't cry that no one tells me to finish my beets!)

Do you like my new "A"s? They are typewriter "A"s. They look like balloons that tripped and fell on their chins. P-o-o-or balloons.

EXPERIMENT

If I stick my tongue out at Matt, he sticks his tongue out at me!

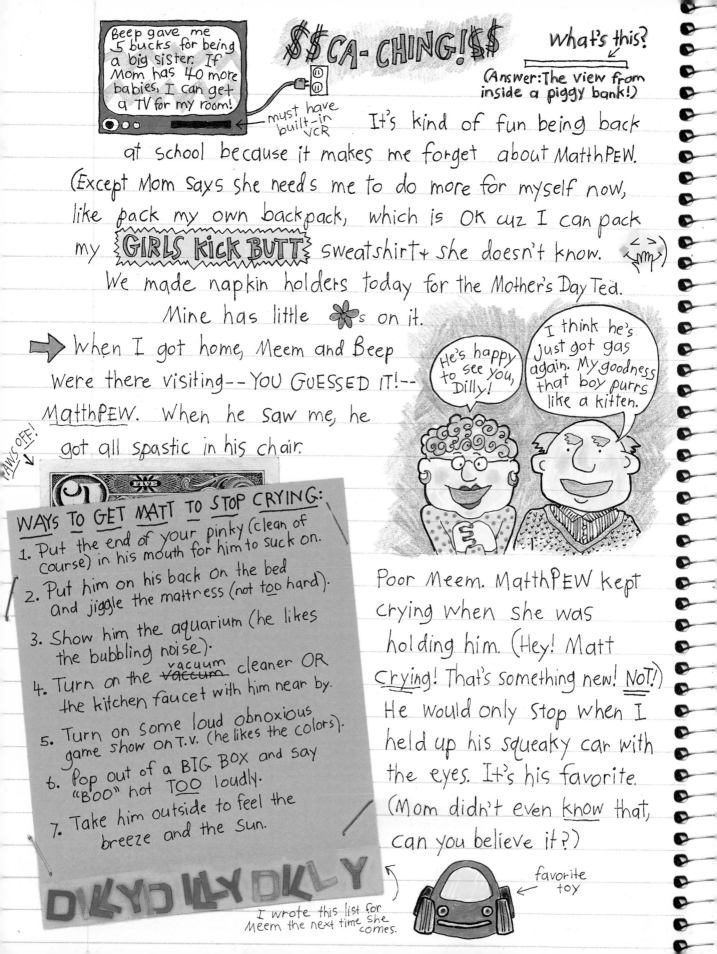

Beep gave me 5 bucks for being a big sister. If Mom has 40 more babies, I can get a TV for my room!

← must have built-in VCR

$$CA-CHING!$$

What's this? ↓
(Answer: The view from inside a piggy bank!)

It's kind of fun being back at school because it makes me forget about MatthPEW. (Except Mom says she needs me to do more for myself now, like pack my own backpack, which is OK cuz I can pack my GIRLS KICK BUTT sweatshirt + she doesn't know. <゚.゚>

We made napkin holders today for the Mother's Day Tea. Mine has little ✿s on it.

➡ When I got home, Meem and Beep were there visiting-- YOU GUESSED IT!-- MatthPEW. When he saw me, he got all spastic in his chair.

PAWS OFF! ↓

He's happy to see you, Dilly!

I think he's just got gas again. My goodness that boy purrs like a kitten.

WAYS TO GET MATT TO STOP CRYING:
1. Put the end of your pinky (clean of course) in his mouth for him to suck on.
2. Put him on his back on the bed and jiggle the mattress (not too hard).
3. Show him the aquarium (he likes the bubbling noise).
4. Turn on the ~~vacuum~~ vacuum cleaner OR the kitchen faucet with him near by.
5. Turn on some loud obnoxious game show on T.V. (he likes the colors).
6. Pop out of a BIG BOX and say "BOO" not TOO loudly.
7. Take him outside to feel the breeze and the sun.

Poor Meem. MatthPEW kept crying when she was holding him. (Hey! Matt crying! That's something new! NOT!) He would only stop when I held up his squeaky car with the eyes. It's his favorite. (Mom didn't even know that, can you believe it?)

DILLY DILLY DILLY

I wrote this list for Meem the next time she comes.

favorite toy ←

HEADLINE NEWS:
BIG SISTER GETS ½ HOUR ADDED TO BEDTIME!

When Mom is doing stuff for MatthPEW and I need her she says "My hands are busy now." I think she read that in a book somewhere. Like if she says, "I can't come now because I'm taking care of your dopey brother," I'd hate him or something.

Today in school we had to write about why our moms are special. (Mrs. Bunn is going to read them aloud at the Mother's Day Tea.) I liked mine best.

← Meredith

My mom is special because she is a doctor and she can fix broken bones and do ~~surgery~~ surgery.

Me →

My mom is special because she meets me at the bus stop every day after school, not just when it's raining like some other moms.

After school I listened to some of the story tapes Mom made for me B.M.   Matt had to listen to these B-O-O-ORING lullaby tapes some old church lady gave him. When Mom was out getting the mail I put on the POLKA FAVORITES tape Beep gave me and hid his lullaby tape in the mending pile where no one goes.   He loved it!

EXPERIMENTS

① When I clap my hands, Matt shuts his eyes.

② He used to like my pictures of circles and stripes but now he likes my face pictures best.

③ His eyes follow the red clown rattle when I hold it sort of close to his face, but he stops looking when I hold it farther away. Hmmm......

I can't wait for the tea tomorrow—brothers and sisters are NOT allowed to come! HEE HEE HEE!!

Just Me and Mom

I can't believe it.

MOM FORGOT ABOUT THE TEA AT SCHOOL

ALL the other mothers came (except for Sam Horton whose father came, probably because his mother is grossed out by him like every other girl). Mrs. Bunn sat next to me and used the placemat I made for Mom. She was very nice to me but it wasn't the same at all.

Mrs. Bunn, trying really hard to be so nice

me, bumming

Meredith and her Mom (in matching dresses, of course)

Even ANNIE'S mother came and SHE owns a restaurant.

Mom came running in at the very end of school all upset. She said that she fell asleep when Matt took a nap and she didn't wake up until the tea was OVER. That little brat has been crying all night and keeping Mom up. She was very, very, very sorry, I could tell, but I'm not sure I can ever forgive her, even when I'm, like, 42.

I WANT MATTHPEW TO FIND A NEW MOTHER AND LEAVE MINE ALONE!!!

(I'm not on fire. These are MAD SPIKES)

I'm still **VERY MAD** at Mom and **VERY, VERY MAD** at stinky old MatthPEW (who is one month old today, Dad says. Big stinkin' deal.)

Dodo Jeffrey sent his postcard back (probably his mother made him):

Kid can't even spell— SHEESH!!

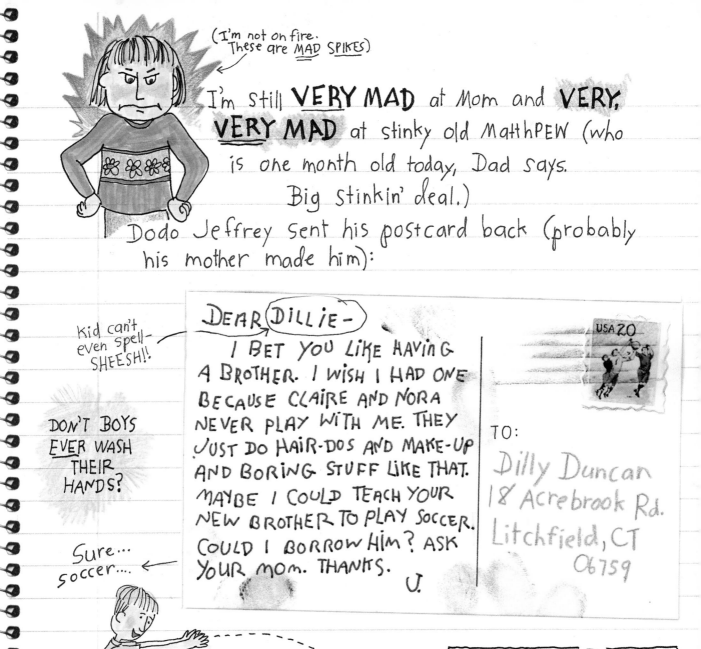

DEAR DILLIE-
I BET YOU LIKE HAVING A BROTHER. I WISH I HAD ONE BECAUSE CLAIRE AND NORA NEVER PLAY WITH ME. THEY JUST DO HAIR-DOS AND MAKE-UP AND BORING STUFF LIKE THAT. MAYBE I COULD TEACH YOUR NEW BROTHER TO PLAY SOCCER. COULD I BORROW HIM? ASK YOUR MOM. THANKS.
J.

USA 20

TO:
Dilly Duncan
18 Acrebrook Rd.
Litchfield, CT
06759

DON'T BOYS EVER WASH THEIR HANDS?

Sure... soccer....

"Kick it!"

BOINK!

WAAAAA

eww

Spit up. Gross me out.

Yeah, Jeff. I'll send him RIGHT over.
(Duh! He was just born.)

Gotta go. Mom wants to talk to me. I'm **NOT** going to forgive her **NO MATTER WHAT.**

I tried REALLY hard to stay angry at Mom, but I couldn't. She had made all of these EXCELLENT plans for us. We had a SPECIAL TEA on the REAL MOTHER'S DAY just for us and Meredith and her mom. First (and BEST) of all, Dad took Matt to Meem and Beep's house so we could have some PEACE & QUIET. Then Mom and ~~me~~ I oops made scones and pecan tassies from Meem's recipe. We made REAL HOT tea and used Great Gram's china tea cups and fancy little dishes.

We decorated with streamers!

Meredith and her Mom wore their matching dresses

POLKA FAVORITES!

me, in fancy clothes from the dress-up closet (and Mom curled my hair!)

Real tea!

Real cream and sugar

It was <u>way</u> more fun than the one at school because at school I got stuck sitting with Sam Horton and Blaine (who both make gross eating noises). PLUS our school tea was in the library and Mrs. Gerchman the librarian was all worried about us spilling on her new carpet. And she kept telling us to use our listening ears and our inside voices.

SHHHHH

when Dad brought Matt back, Meredith's Mom held him and got all mushy. Meredith said, "Don't get me one of those!" and her mother turned all red.

WAAAAA NA NA poke poke PTHHHT

MY LIFE AS A BIG SISTER FOR THE NEXT 75 YEARS

This afternoon Dad and I took Matt for a walk while Mom napped. When we passed Beanie's house, Dad said, "Look at Beanie playing in the tree fort with her brothers. It won't be long before Matt can play like that!"

But then I looked at Matt and he started to pull his own hair which made him cry and then he spit up all over his blanket.

And it seems like it will be a <u>VERY</u> long time.

spit up. Gross me out.

So far the only game we play is
← STARING CONTEST

He plays pretty hard, but I <u>always</u> win!

HA HA! Now <u>MATTHEW</u> knows what it's like to wait!

Mom was still napping when we got home so Dad and I started to play CRAZY EIGHTS. Matt started- <u>WHAT ELSE</u> — **BAWLING.**

Forget the game, Dad. Go ahead and deal with him.

No, we'll finish this game. He can wait a minute.

→ And pretty soon he stopped crying all on his own and started playing with his toes or some other weird baby game.

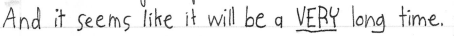

AND **I** WON THE CARD GAME!
(And Dad was re<u>all</u>y trying!)

SPECIAL ANNOUNCEMENT

Matt smiled his first __REAL__ smile at **ME!**

(It was actually a very cute smile, even for a little stinker like him! ☺)

The rest of the postcards have all come back to me now →

DEAR DILLY,
CONGRAJULASHUNS! ← (I don't think that is spelled right so don't show. Mrs. Bunn)
YOU ARE LUCKY YOU'RE THE OLDEST. I BET YOUR BROTHER WON'T TAKE YOUR SPARKLY NAIL POLISH AND YOUR FAVORITE FLIP-FLOPS LIKE MY SISTER. I BET YOUR BROTHER WON'T TRAIN YOUR BUNNY TO BITE YOU AND TAKE THE PURPLE GUMBALLS OUT OF YOUR GUMBALL MACHINE WITHOUT ASKING. BUT CONGRAJU.... ANYWAY. HAVING A BROTHER OR SISTER IS O.K. REALLY KIND OF ~~FUN~~. YOUR FRIEND, Annie

TO:
Dilly Duncan
18 Acrebrook Rd.
Litchfield, CT.
06759

USA 20

Dear Dilly,
I have a little b
His name is Jack a
likes dinosaurs. H
play with because h
cool toys like castle blocks
and he will play games like
cave under the stairs that
my friends think are too baby.
So having a litt
is pretty cool
See you on the
Love,
Cammy

"KNOCK-KNOCK!"
"Who's there?"
"Jamaica!"
"Jamaica who?"
"Jamaica my bacon sandwich yet?"

TO:
Dilly Duncan
18 Acrebrook Rd
Litchfield CT

Dear Dilly,
I have never written to you because you live next door. It seems weird. I hope you don't mind if I took off the stamp to save and I'll put this in your mailbox myself. I want to be a mailman LADY when I grow up so it will be good practice. Or maybe I might be a vet except that I DO NOT LIKE __COWS__. They smell __very__ bad. Love, Guess who?

TO:
Dilly Duncan
18 Acrebrook Rd.
Litchfield, CT.
06759

P.S. Good news about matthew - I've got a ton of brothers and it's not as bad as it sounds.

Cool button I found on the playground

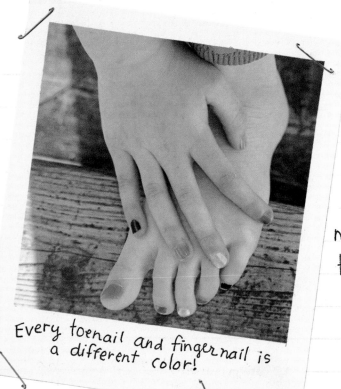

Every toenail and fingernail is a different color!

For Mother's Day, Dad gave Mom an I.O.U. for a MANICURE and a PEDICURE. She wanted to go today with ME! When she told me it meant finger-nail and toenail polish and I got to pick the color, I said, "Yipee!"

me, → BABY POLICE!

wobbly wheeled car

HELLO Meem! Didn't you have babies of your own so you're supposed to know this stuff? He could swallow this wheel!

Meem stayed with Matt while we went. Can you believe she let him play with a little car with a wobbly wheel? AM I THE ONLY ONE WHO KNOWS ANYTHING ABOUT BABIES??

I put myself in charge of checking the toys in Matt's basket. Look at what I took out!

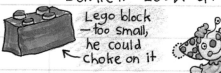

Lego block —too small, he could choke on it

Eye falling off (plus I hate clowns— Bye bye!)

sharp corners— BAD NEWS !!

GOOD BOY. YUCKY YUCKY CHEESE!

EXPERIMENT

stinky cheese   Mom's perfume

See? He always looks at Mom's perfume! His nose works!!

You are my favorite daughter! ♡ Mom

Meredith made me SO MAD at school today!!!! She found a little tiny heart charm at the bus stop and gave it to [ME]. Then she sat with Beanie in the front seat of the bus and told me to give it BACK so she could give it to Beanie!

Beanie

NO! I won't give it back!

Then you're NOT my best friend anymore!

Uh oh.

My own riddle: SMELL on the playground? Why do teachers they're ON DUTY! (On DOODY, get it?)

Meredith was so RUDE to me all through morning meeting, S.S.R., and snack and chapter book. At recess, she played with Annie, Beanie and Cammy and looked at me, whispering. I kept Mrs. Bunn company on her playground duty. I think Meredith told the whole class weird stories about me because everyone looked at me all day like I was mental. It was a l-o-o-o-ng day.

Even if Matt gets really mad at me someday, he can't say he won't be my brother anymore. He's stuck with me just like I'm stuck with him.

(Thank goodness Mom and Matt were waiting at the bus stop for me.)

← heart charm still in my pocket! HA!

I'M GLAD TODAY IS OVER

Matt was sort of fussy when we got home so Mom let me put SLIMY vegetable oil on my hands and give him a baby massage like we saw in a book. Afterward, he fell right to sleep. zzz Mom and I high-fived each other! Then Mom videotaped me doing the Chicken Dance. (Matt misses me when I'm at school!)

HELLO!

Did everyone FORGET SOMETHING?
(or SomeONE?)

I was the **ONLY** one who gave him any presents! (AND HE **LOVED** THEM, of course!)

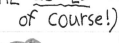

MATT is 2 MONTHS OLD!!

Uncooked rice in plastic container that he likes to hear me shake

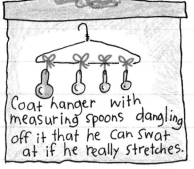

Coat hanger with measuring spoons dangling off it that he can swat at if he really stretches.

Blinky Christmas lights I found in the attic to wrap around the handle of Matt's baby seat for him to look at.

Actually, Matt's favorite toy is his own hand. The thing is, he doesn't know that it's **HIS** hand!

"Hey! What's that cool thing?"

Oh my!

OUCH!

WAAAAH!

Hey *SNIFF* What's **THAT** thing?

Hey! I almost forgot the BEST PART OF THE DAY!

BEST FRIENDS 4 EVER!

YOURS 'TIL BUTTER FLIES!

Meredith called just before I left for the bus and said she was sorry and I could keep the heart. ♡ (Then at school her mom packed RAISINS 😬 for her snack so I shared my GUMMY SHARKS 🐟 with her.) GOOD THING we made up fast cuz summer is ALMOST HERE! It would have been a L-O-O-O-N-G summer with no Meredith!

Sorry I'm not writing EVERYDAY in this diary but between school, gymnastics, playing and this BIG SISTER thing, I'm kind of busy.

Carrie ("LUV") came again so Mom and Dad could go out to dinner in a restaurant. THIS TIME Mom and Dad told her to **LISTEN** to ME! Right away she put Matt down on his back to play and he started hollering.

He hates being on his back because that's how Mom puts him down to nap so he thinks you want him to nap. You have to put him on his stomach.

Of course as soon as she took my advice, he stopped crying! Then he saw me and he started REALLY smiling and gurgling and jerking his little arms + legs around.

MATT: U R A QT!

Carrie
Hi Matt!
me
Hi Matty! It's me!

EXPERIMENT

I think this girl Dilly will make QUITE a scientist!

When Carrie talked to Matt, he frowned and turned away. When I talked to him, he looked right at me. I told Carrie not to have her feelings hurt, it's just that she's a stranger. I don't want to make Mom and Dad feel bad either, but Matt really likes me best.

I don't think I should do too many summer camps this year. Matt really needs me around.

SCHOOL'S OUT FOR THE WHOLE LO-O-ONG SUMMER!!!

Bye Mrs. Bunn!

Dad says that he'll buy a pool deep enough to go UNDERWATER in— YEA!! I told Meredith and Beanie they could come over and swim with me ANYTIME they want to!

Dad brought home MORE pictures...

Meredith and me ———————→

← See? I gave him back the shark!

When I was pushing Matt in the stroller today (which, by the way, I get 50¢ for), Beanie and her brothers were outside playing. One of her brothers was BURPING a song. It was SO GROSS. Matt will NEVER be like that. I'll shape him into a nice boy.

BURP
BURP
BURP

SO FUN!

The summer is starting out **SO FUN!** Tomorrow is going to be very <u>hot</u>, so Dad is taking us to the beach — the <u>REAL</u> beach with waves and sea gulls and **SILKY WHITE SAND!** Best of all...

MEREDITH IS COMING!

Now I like my hair like this!

Matt doesn't cry as much anymore, which makes him <u>way</u> more **FUN!** If we put him on his tummy, he can hold his head up. (It looks like a lot of work. It is a BIG head.)

He looks like he could crawl soon, but Dad said not until Christmas time. He said that I could put LOCKS with real keys on my Christmas list. That will keep Matt out of my important stuff. Dad said he'd help me make a big **CUT-OUT** of **ME** to put on my door so Matt will know he's not supposed to go in without <u>knocking</u>.

WHAT WE THINK HE'S THINKING

$4N=a$
$64\overline{)5,483,8}$
$<92>2\times180=$
$=H_2O+C$

I NEED A NEW LOOK...

← WHAT HE'S REALLY THINKING

EXPERIMENT

Matt likes my REAL FACE more than my photo.

(He used to like BOTH the same.)

The summer didn't start out too FUN for Matt. He had to go to the doctor's for a check-up and a <u>**SHOT**</u>. Poor kid. He never saw that needle coming. But I cheered him up QUICK with the ♪ **CHICKEN DANCE!** ♪

This is my favorite dress — I never, ever get sick of it.